Praise for *The Presidents Did What?*

"I loved *The Presidents Did What?* As a father of seven and a history buff, I loved how the book found a unique way to teach and keep kids interested in history. I knew my kids would love it, but I wasn't prepared for the meaningful conversations we had after reading the book. This book will stay on our bookshelf as my boys get older."

—Matt Paxton, father of seven children and host of the hit shows *Legacy List with Matt Paxton* and *Hoarders*

"In *The Presidents Did What?*, Wag Harrison takes us on an educational and entertaining journey through the White House while meeting up with some of its least distinguished inhabitants."

—Gregory McAlpin, EdS, Virginia Beach City Public Schools

"In these pages, Harrison deftly underscores the most valuable of these sentiments using figures who reached new lows while held to history's highest standards. *The Presidents Did What?* quite literally brings to life a rogues' gallery of our nation's disgraced presidents, framing their most egregious misdeeds in fascinating historical perspective. Combining clever wit, imaginative storytelling, and an informed understanding of the ghosts of presidents past, Harrison shows us that sometimes the biggest mistakes teach the most valuable lessons."

—Brett C. Brown, stay-at-home dad, person of consequence

"In the tale *The Presidents Did What?* by Wag Harrison, the ghost of President Millard Fillmore takes readers on a journey through the White House to speak to the other ghosts of one-term presidents. Here, Fillmore and other presidents, such as Martin Van Buren and Warren G. Harding, hash out the flaws and mistakes that ruined their chances at a second term. Not only did I learn a thing or two, but I found myself fully engaged in this children's book even as an adult. This children's book is one for the history books, literally, and belongs on everyone's shelf."

—Lori Starling, MFA, author of *Toby Wears a Tutu*

THE PRESIDENTS DID WHAT?

STORY BY

WAG HARRISON

ILLUSTRATIONS BY

C. ROD. UNALT

BELLE ISLE BOOKS
www.belleislebooks.com

ISBN: 978-1-953021-33-5
LCCN: 2021911405

Designed by Michael Hardison
Project Managed by Grace Ball

Printed in the United States of America

Published by
Belle Isle Books (an imprint of Brandylane Publishers, Inc.)
5 S. 1st Street
Richmond, Virginia 23219

BELLE ISLE BOOKS
www.belleislebooks.com

belleislebooks.com | brandylanepublishers.com

For Devon

May God save the country, for it is evident that the people will not.

—President Millard Fillmore

If you think today's president is dreadful, you should learn about yesterday's.

—*Ghost President Millard Fillmore*

"Hello, my friend! Welcome to the White House. I am Millard Fillmore, the 13th president of the United States—you can call me Milly, if you wish. Now, please don't be alarmed. Indeed, I am a ghost. Why am I, both formerly a president and currently a ghost, giving tours of the White House? A fine question! You see, nearly all one-term presidents, such as I, were one-term presidents because we made very poor, indeed disastrous, decisions during our years in office. As a consequence of our failings, we are now forced to spend our afterlives giving tours of this Executive Mansion. We think of this as our opportunity to finally give back to the good people of this great land—good people like you, my friend. Now, mind you, I am not quite sure who is making us do this, but here we are nonetheless. Let's get started!" Fillmore turns on his heel and leads the way through the Entrance Hall. "Today, you will meet several former presidents, and you will hear about the decisions we made during our respective terms. I do hope you find us both entertaining and enlightening."

President Fillmore slows and comes to a stop. "Before we arrive at the first room on our tour, friend, I'd like to address the proverbial elephant in the living room—might you be wondering what poor decisions I made during my presidency? Well, I very much regret signing a law that ensured runaway slaves were returned to their masters. I also, admittedly, held a strong belief that immigrants should not be allowed entry into the United States," he says.

"Now friend, I was always opposed to slavery, but the Fugitive Slave Act was part of the Compromise of 1850 that held the country together a bit longer before the Civil War. Nonetheless, signing that law was a dreadful decision. Regarding my misguided stance on immigration—I know you may be an immigrant, or your parents may have been immigrants, and so on and so forth. Should I want you to leave? Oh, no! Most certainly not!" says Fillmore. "You are most welcome. I am truly sorry for my former actions and beliefs. I was a 'Know-Nothing' then, and now know, my friend, I was wrong. I am truly and deeply sorry.

"Are we still quite good? Yes? Wonderful! Now please join me, and we will begin our tour properly," says Fillmore. He turns once again and leads the way across the hall.

"Our first stop is the Red Room," says Fillmore, gesturing to the red walls and matching plush furniture. "This room has been used as a music room by a number of our presidents and their families. Ah, and today we find our most musical president, Warren G. Harding."

"I played nearly every instrument, but one of my favorites was the tuba," says President Harding.

"Indeed, our 29th president also played poker—lots of poker, in fact—and he appointed his crooked poker buddies to important Cabinet positions. How did that play out for you, Warren?" asks Fillmore.

"I got played, Milly. My friends messed up everything awful bad, lied a bunch, and robbed the country of a great deal of money," says Harding.

"You chose bad pals, Warren," says Fillmore.

"I did. I had no trouble with my enemies, but my friends kept me walking the floors at night. And I was a fairly bad husband to boot. I feel just awful about all of it," says Harding.

"You do sound quite remorseful, Warren," says Fillmore.

BLOOOOERMP, responds Harding on the tuba.

"Well said. Thank you for that, Warren." says Fillmore. "Let's move along, shall we?"

President Fillmore closes the Red Room door behind him, quieting the sounds of the tuba, and walks just a couple steps to the next stop on the tour. "Here we have The State Dining Room. This room hosts leaders from around the world in both good times and bad. Speaking of bad times, here is Herbert Hoover, our 31st president. Hoover served during the Great Depression. President Hoover, when you were campaigning, you promised Americans a chicken in every pot. Do I have that correct?"

"And a car in every garage. Yes, I remember," says Hoover, holding his chin in one hand and a chicken leg in the other. "Alas, after the stock market crashed, all those people lost their jobs, and all the banks closed their doors. I did not keep my promise. There were no chickens and no cars for anyone. Many Americans lost everything they had, and I did nothing. I wanted the American people to get themselves out of the Great Depression. You see, I thought that if I helped them, they'd never learn to help themselves."

"So, you didn't lend a helping hand to millions of struggling Americans, nearly all suffering through no fault of their own, on principle?" asks Fillmore.

"Indeed," says Hoover. "But I have since seen the light. I didn't help then, but I want to help now! Look here, you can have some of this chicken. You can put it in your pot now, can't you?" Hoover holds out the drumstick.

"Oh, dear goodness. There is, I'm sad to say, little hope for you, Herbert," says Fillmore. He looks past President Hoover, down the hall. "Let's move along and see who is in the Blue Room. Come on, then, here we go!" he says.

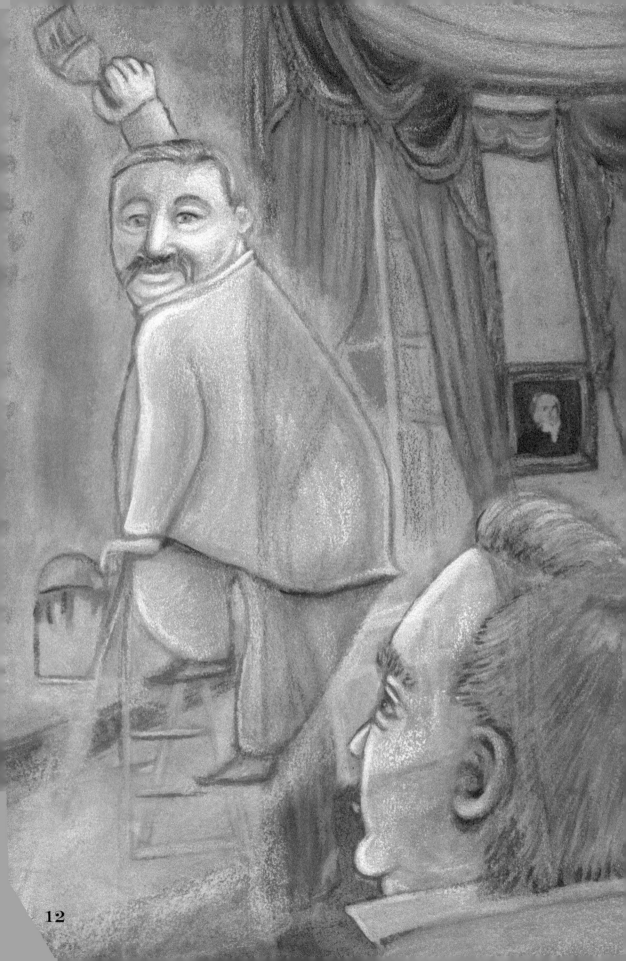

"Originally painted blue by Louis Tiffany, the beautiful Blue Room is used for receptions and ceremonies. Here, in 1886, President Grover Cleveland became the only president to get married in the White House. And dear me! Here he is—our 22nd and 24th president—the only president to serve non-consecutive terms of office. Greetings, Big Steve!"

"Fillmore! You know I don't belong here. I was a two-term president," says Cleveland.

"Now, Big Steve, we've been over this hundreds of times," says Fillmore. "You were a one-term president *twice*."

"Again, I insist I do not belong here, Fillmore!" shouts Cleveland.

"But, alas, here you are—and for good reason. Please, do give that ladder a sorely needed break and take a moment to enlighten us," says Fillmore.

"Well, you and your friend may have one moment and one only, so here it goes: I supported and signed the Dawes Act," says President Cleveland. "This act was designed to help Native Americans assimilate into American society. Well, the result was disastrous. The Dawes Act took away their land, destroyed their cultures and traditions, and devastated their way of life."

Cleveland leans against the wall for support.

"Can this be true, Big Steve?" asks Fillmore.

"It is completely true—what a terrible thing to do. I am so very sorry," says Cleveland.

"Why, you are certainly looking quite blue. Thank you for your moment. You are bursting with remorse and generosity—just as you should be. Come, friend, on to our next stop—just one door down," says Fillmore.

"This is the Green Room. This room has seen the signing of a declaration of war, has been used for funerals, and has hosted card games," says Fillmore. "But mostly, it's used as a cocktail lounge. Accordingly, here is Andrew Johnson, our 17th president. A slave owner who later opposed citizenship for former slaves, President Johnson was our first president to be impeached. When confronted with the issue of bringing our country back together after the Civil War, President Johnson met that challenge with a record number of vetoes and, most likely, a record number of stiff brandies. Doesn't that sound right, Andy?"

"You flerp jibit! Not true, snot none vit!" stammers Johnson.

"Aren't you feeling well, Andy?" asks Fillmore, eyeing the peach liquor bottle under Johnson's arm.

"Yessir. Juss fline. Yep, from Tennessee. My wife teach me read. Then floop! Ole Abe was a gonner. Then they gonna veto me? You not gonna veto me. No sir! I'm gonna veto you! Yep, will have none vit. Bye!" says Johnson, sinking back into his chair.

"Good enough, Andy. Exactly as I would have explained the situation, I assure you. Quickly, now—let's go and see who we can find in the next room on our tour," says Fillmore.

"This reception hall is called the East Room. It has been the location of many historic events, including the signing of treaties, presidential funerals, and swearing-in ceremonies. The East Room is the largest room in the White House, and yet, it now hosts the smallest of men, President James Buchanan."

"Still sour about the 1856 election, are you, Milly?" asks Buchanan, grinning.

"Jim, here, defeated me in the 1856 election to become our 15th president. *I* may have lost the election, but how did those four years go for *you*, Jim?" asks Fillmore.

President Buchanan frowns. "Well, some of my decisions may have—"

"Allow me, Jim," Fillmore interrupts. "You see, President Buchanan sat idly by as our nation dissolved. He allowed the Southern states to secede from the United States with hardly a murmur of concern. Jim was a supporter of slavery, so he did absolutely nothing to save the country from a civil war. Yes, Jim is widely regarded as the worst president this country has ever had."

"Beg your pardon, Milly," says Buchanan, "I *was* regarded as the worst president. Thankfully, it appears that I am no longer considered as such. I am now simply amongst the worst presidents—just like you, Milly."

"Well, congrats from us, Jim. Quite the accomplishment," says Fillmore, rolling his eyes. "But now, come along, friend. Let's leave Jim alone. We've got a bit of walking to do to get to our next stop. Shall we?"

18

Fillmore leads the way to the ground level of the White House. "Ah, yes. Here we are! Welcome to the China Room," says Fillmore. "At one point, a fireman slept in this room. President Martin Van Buren hired him to keep the White House furnace going. Now it houses our collection of each president's fine china dinnerware. And here is Martin Van Buren, our 8th president. Now, Marty, why all the tears?" asks Fillmore, patting a sobbing Van Buren on the shoulder.

"I am crying because I cannot stop," says President Van Buren. "A long time ago, in 1838, I ordered the US Army to remove all members of the Cherokee Nation from their homes in Georgia and force them to walk hundreds of miles to a reservation in Oklahoma. Not only did they lose their homes and land, but a great many of these good and proud people died along the way. Their journey became known as the Trail of Tears."

"That is not OK, Marty," says Fillmore.

"Well I know that now!" says Van Buren.

"Perhaps that's so, Marty, but unfortunately, that doesn't do much good. Ah, look here, friend—we have a delightful surprise!" says Fillmore. "Chester A. Arthur, our 21st president, has decided to join us."

"Fillmore, I am here every single day. You know this. This is not a surprise," says President Arthur.

"Of course, you are correct, Chet," says Fillmore. "Please do remind us why you are here every single day."

"I will not, for I am busy," says Arthur.

"Doing a dandy job, indeed. Please, President Arthur, won't you tell us why you are cleaning the china?" asks Fillmore.

"If I must. Fine china dinnerware is named after its country of origin," says Arthur. "While president, I signed a law that said Chinese people were no longer allowed to move to the United States. This was the first time the United States banned immigrants from a specific country. The law lasted for well over sixty years. That awful, racist decision is why I have to spend my afterlife cleaning this china," he says, waving his hand across the china cabinet next to him.

"Do beg my pardon, but you don't seem too remorseful, Chet," says Fillmore.

"I have no time to wallow—not like crybaby over there, anyway. But I assure you I would sooner request that every single person living in China come here to America than wash another plate," says President Arthur, setting down the piece he'd been polishing. "I also assure you I am sad and sorry I signed that law. And finally, I assure you that YOU know I will be here tomorrow, and still, YOU will act surprised to see me," says Arthur in a huff. He picks up another plate and gets back to work.

"Indeed," says Fillmore. "Well, hope to see you tomorrow, Chet! Come along now, friend," says Fillmore, stepping back through the doorway. "Let's take a quick trip to the West Wing."

President Fillmore leads the way through the Palm Room and down the West Colonnade, stopping outside a pair of doors at the end. "Worth noting," says Fillmore. "Just inside here is the Oval Office. That is the office space for the sitting president. However, we are not able . . ."

TWEET! TWEET! GRRR! TWEET! GRRRR! TWEET!

"Hmmm. Now, I assure you there are no birds or dogs in the Oval Office. The Commander in Chief is simply . . . how to say this . . . working ardently and diligently to achieve national greatness," says Fillmore. "I know you may be inclined to meet this president now. Unfortunately, that is out of the question. However, chin up. If you return for a tour on a future date, you may very well have the opportunity."

President Fillmore leads the way back to the Entrance Hall. "Alas, we have come to the end of our tour, my friend," says Fillmore. "Please allow me to personally thank you for your delightful company and mindful attention. You have no doubt heard many sorrowful tales. Are you saddened by them? Indeed! It is hard to fathom the dreadful things our presidents have done to so many people!

"However horrific, my friend, it is so very important to hear these stories. You see, a long time ago, President George Washington said that there is no point in looking back through history unless to learn from mistakes. This is very sound advice. These sad stories are our lessons. We are only strong if we understand our weaknesses. We will only find success if we learn from our failures. Do you understand? It is my hope that you have learned something today. We can and *must* do better! You can see to it, my friend. You can make your voice heard and, one day, make your vote count—you may very well save this country yet.

"On that note, friend, I wish you well. Good day, and good luck to you."

ABOUT THE AUTHOR

Wag Harrison is an award-winning writer and educator. Holding graduate degrees in both history and educational leadership, Wag spent nearly twenty years as a teacher and school administrator before settling in as a full-time father. A lifelong lover of learning and of telling tales from the past, Wag is proud to call *The Presidents Did What?* his flagship picture book. Wag lives in Bon Air, Virginia, with his wife and three children.

ABOUT THE ILLUSTRATOR

Christina Rodriguez-Unalt, or "C. Rod. Unalt," is an illustrator of all things whimsical. She's been creating images since her kindergarten teacher taught her how to use a scratchboard and has been working professionally for over a decade. Christina began her career as a scenic painter at a creature shop, where she painted murals and large-scale sculptures for mini golf courses, storefronts, windows, and parade floats. Her work has appeared in children's magazines and textbooks, and she holds a master's degree in illustration. This is her fourth illustrated book.

CPSIA information can be obtained
at www.ICGtesting.com
Printed in the USA
LVHW071027031022
729819LV00006B/22